THE
CORAL ISLAND

— R. M. Ballantyne —

THE
CORAL ISLAND

PETER HADDOCK PUBLISHING

Published in this edition 1997 by Peter Haddock Publishing,
United Kingdom
Reprinted 1999, 2004

© 1997 This arrangement, text and illustrations,
Geddes & Grosset, David Dale House,
New Lanark, Scotland

© Original text John Kennett

Illustrated by Ray Mutimer (Simon Girling Associates)

ISBN 0 7105 0930 8

Printed and bound in Poland

Contents

To the Reader

I am sure you will have seen a film, or watched a programme on TV, that has been made from some famous book. If you enjoyed the film or programme, you may have decided to read the book.

Then what happens? You get the book and, it's more than likely, you get a shock as well! You turn ten or twenty pages, and nothing seems to *happen*. Where are all the lively people and exciting incidents? When, you say, will the author get down to telling the story? In the end you will probably throw the book aside and give it up. Now, why is that?

Well, perhaps the author was writing for adults and not for children. Perhaps the book was written a long time ago, when people had more time for reading and liked nothing better than a book that would keep them entertained for weeks.

We think differently today. That's why I've taken some of these wonderful books, and retold them for you. If you enjoy them in this shorter form, then I hope that when you are older you will go back to the original books, and enjoy all the more the wonderful stories they have to tell.

About the Author

Robert Michael Ballantyne, born in Edinburgh in 1825, was a nephew of James Ballantyne, who printed the works of Sir Walter Scott. From 1841 to 1848 he was employed as a clerk in Canada under the Hudson's Bay Fur Company, and for the next seven years he was in the service of Thomas Constable, the Edinburgh publisher and printer. In 1855 he began his long series of books of adventure with *The Young Fur Traders*. *The Coral Island* was published in 1857. He died at Rome in 1894.

Chapter One
The Wreck

For three days and nights our ship had driven before the storm, and now the end was near. Death looked us in the face.

There could be no doubt of that. The ship was breaking up. The first blast of the gale had carried away two of our masts: the frightful walls of water that came sweeping across the Pacific Ocean had torn off our rudder and left us at the mercy of wind and waves. Everything had been swept off the decks except one small boat, and we had been blown far out of our course. I knew that we might find ourselves among dangerous coral reefs—and I, Ralph Rover, fifteen years old and mad about the sea, was terribly afraid.

Then, at the dawn of the third day, there came a cry from the look-out:

"Land! Land ahead!"

I tried to peer through the sheeted rain. Its drops struck at me like bullets. I had never dreamed it could blow so hard. The wind was a screaming fury that rushed in through my mouth and strangled me as I faced it . . .

And then the ship rose on a mountainous wave, and I saw the dark mass of land that lay ahead. It was an island, encircled by a reef of pounded coral on which the waves were breaking in a fury of flying foam. There was calm water within the reef, but I could see only one narrow opening into the lagoon. My heart sank. We had no chance of winning through without a rudder.

I felt hopeless.

I turned my head and stared at the two boys who clung to the rigging beside me. There were three of us serving as apprentices on board the *Arrow*: Jack Martin, a tall, strong lad of eighteen, Peterkin Gay, who was little and quick and funny, and about fourteen years old, and myself. Even in that awful moment, Jack's face showed no sign of fear, though Peterkin looked sick and scared, and there were tears of pain in his eyes from the hard slaps of wind and spray, and the long driving spears of rain.

Above the roar of the gale I heard the captain give a shout.

"It's all up with us, lads! Stand by to launch the boat! We'll be on the rocks any minute now!"

Jack grabbed hold of my arm.

"Never mind the boat!" he screamed in my ear. "It's sure to upset in this. When I give the word, make a dash for it and grab that big oar in the bows. If it's driven over the breakers we might get to the shore."

I shouted an answer, and clung on, as a great wall of water caught the ship, tilted her over at a crazy angle, and flung her towards the reef. I looked at the white waves that lashed the reef and boiled against its rocks, and had little hope of coming through alive.

Things happened quickly.

Wind and the heaving seas were shoving the *Arrow* towards the reef. I saw the men standing by the boat and the

captain beside them giving orders. The reef was very close, and a tremendous wave was rushing towards us.

"Now!" Jack yelled.

We clawed our way towards the bows, clinging to the rigging, and sobbing for air as we leaned into the wind. The wave fell on the deck with a crash like thunder. A rush of water went over my head. As I clung desperately to the rigging, the ship struck; the foremast broke off close to the deck and went over the side, carrying the boat and men with it. I saw the sea churned to flying foam; I had a glimpse of black heads and upflung arms silhouetted against the frothing white of the waves, and then all of them vanished.

We three ran towards the bow to lay hold of our oar. It was entangled with the wreck, and Jack seized an axe to cut it free. A lurch of the ship made him miss the ropes and he struck the axe deep into the oar. Another wave washed it clear of the wreck. We all seized hold of it. Wind and water caught it and whirled it away, and the next instant we were struggling in the wild sea.

I felt myself lifted and driven through the air, and then I dropped like a stone. A rush of salt water went over my head. I was drowning. I could no longer breathe. Again the waves lifted me and hurled me forward. I crashed down and something struck my head a heavy blow. I pitched headfirst into a watery darkness.

Chapter Two
The Island

I felt water splashing on my face. I slowly opened my eyes.

I was lying, out of the wind, under an overhanging shelf of rock. Peterkin and Jack were kneeling beside me, their faces pale and drawn, and in that moment it all came back to me. I sat up, then blinked and clenched my brows in a frown of pain. I put a hand to my head and found that it had been gashed across.

"Don't rush things, Ralph," said Jack. "You're not quite better yet. Wet your lips with this water. I got it from a spring."

"What—what happened," I asked, "after we were thrown into the water?"

"The oar struck your head," said Jack. "I managed to grab you and push you towards the shore. It wasn't too hard because the water was quite calm inside the reef."

"And the others?" I asked.

Jack shook his head.

"No sign of them," he said quietly.

We were silent for a minute or two.

"Did you see what happened to the ship?" I asked at last.

"She's gone to the bottom," Jack replied. "She struck on the tail of the island and stove in her bow. The next breaker swung her clear, and she floated away to leeward before she filled and went down."

There was a longer silence while we thought about it all. For my part, I did not feel very happy. We might be on a desert island, but if it should turn out to be inhabited I felt certain, from all I had heard of South Sea Islanders, that we should be roasted alive and eaten. If, on the other hand, it should turn out to be uninhabited, I fancied that we might well starve to death.

Jack must have been thinking the same.

"If this is a desert island," he said suddenly, "we'll have to live like wild animals. We haven't a tool of any kind— not even a knife."

Peterkin's face lit up.

"Yes we have!" he cried, and fumbled in his trousers pockets, from which he drew out a small penknife with only one blade—and that was broken.

Jack grinned suddenly.

"Well, that's better than nothing," he said. "Let's see what else we've got."

I sat up. I was feeling a lot better now. My friends had taken off some of their clothes and spread them out in the sun. They had also stripped off most of my wet clothes and laid them out to dry.

We went through our pockets and discovered that we had, between us, the broken penknife, an old silver pencil-case without any lead in it, a piece of cord about six yards long, a small sailmaker's needle, and a ship's telescope.

And that was all!

Jack suddenly started and exclaimed:

"The oar! We've forgotten the oar!"

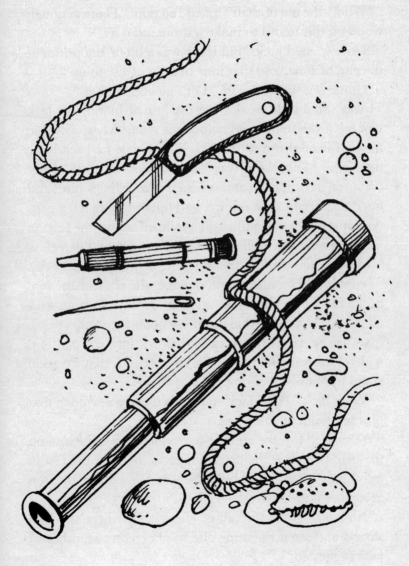

"What's the use of that?" asked Peterkin. "There's enough wood on this island to make a thousand oars."

"I know," said Jack, "but there was a bit of hoop-iron at the end of ours, and that may be a lot of use to us."

"Come on, then," I said. "Let's go and fetch it."

I was still a little weak from the loss of blood, but Jack lent me his shoulder and helped me along. My spirits rose as we walked down to the beach. The gale had suddenly died away. The island was hilly and covered with richly coloured trees and shrubs. A beach of dazzling white sand lined this bright green shore, and upon it there fell a gentle ripple of the sea, although a mile off across the lagoon the great seas were rolling in and crashing upon the reef, to be dashed into white foam and flung up in clouds of spray.

Peterkin ran on ahead and down to the edge of the sea. Suddenly he gave a shout, and we saw him tugging with all his might at something that lay upon the shore.

It was the axe which Jack had struck into the oar, and which had remained fast—so fast, indeed, that Peterkin could not budge it.

"What luck!" cried Jack, and gave the axe a wrench that plucked it out of the wood.

We carried the axe and the oar, which had some iron on the blade, back to the place where we had left the rest of our things, intending to burn the wood away from the iron at a more convenient time.

"Now let's go to the tail of the island, where the ship struck, and see if anything else has been thrown ashore," Jack suggested.

We set off.

"What are we going to eat?" asked Peterkin, as we moved along the white beach. "I could do with a drink, too."

"Look up there," answered Jack, "and you'll see both food and drink."

He pointed to the branched head of a coconut palm, heavily laden with fruit. Peterkin gave a cry of delight and climbed up the tall stem of the tree as easily as a squirrel. In a matter of seconds he had thrown down more than a dozen nuts.

"Now let's have some of the green, unripe ones," Jack called up to him—and down they came, followed by Peterkin.

We cut holes in the unripe nuts with Peterkin's knife and drank gratefully of their cool, sweet milk.

"Marvellous!" cried Peterkin, in high delight. "This is the life! It's like Paradise!"

We went on until we came to the point of rocks off which the ship had struck, and searched carefully along the shore. We found nothing.

The sun was sinking when we walked back. As long as the daylight lasted we worked hard cutting down boughs and leaves and used them to build a sort of wall all round us; then we covered the inner floor with leaves and dry grass. On these we sat down and made our supper from the meat of coconuts.

All of us were yawning by the time we had finished, and we were glad to lie back under the overhanging palms.

That night the starry sky looked down upon our sleep, and the distant roaring of the surf upon the reef was our lullaby.

Chapter Three

A Strange Discovery

I was awakened by a loud scream. I sat up, startled. There came a roar of laughter from Jack and Peterkin, who were already on their feet and looking down at me.

"Wh—what was it?" I stammered.

"A parrot," said Peterkin. "It's been sitting on a twig above your head, looking into your mouth, which was wide open, and wondering if it ought to fly in."

I grinned and rubbed my eyes. The sky was blue and the air heavy with the scent of flowers.

"Who's for a swim?" cried Peterkin.

He began tearing off his clothes, then rushed over the white sands and plunged into the water, even though he could swim only a little, and could not dive at all.

Within ten seconds Jack and I were running after him.

While Peter enjoyed himself in the shallow water, Jack and I swam out into the deep and began diving for stones. The water was so clear that we could see down to a depth of twenty or thirty yards. At our first dive we found ourselves in a kind of submarine garden. The bottom of the lagoon was covered with coral of every size, shape, and hue, through which sported many fishes—blue, red, yellow, green, and striped—and they did not seem to be in the least afraid of us.

After a few minutes, as we both rose to the surface, Jack gave a shout.

"Oysters!" he cried. "Follow me, Ralph."

We dived together. When Jack reached the bottom, he grasped the coral stems and crept along on his hands and knees, peeping under the seaweed and among the rocks. I did the same, and picked up three or four large oysters. Then he sprang like an arrow to the surface, and the two of us swam lazily to the shore.

"Breakfast, Peterkin!" Jack shouted, as we ran up the beach. "Oysters, my boy! Split them open while Ralph and I get dressed."

Peterkin took the oysters and opened them with the edge of our axe.

"This is marvellous!" he exclaimed. "We'll get a fine fire going and roast them for breakfast."

"And how will you start the fire?" I asked.

"Easy!" said Peterkin. "We'll use the end of the telescope as a burning-glass. Leave it to me, my lad."

We left it to him. Inside five minutes he had built up a fire, and we set about roasting our oysters. They tasted delicious.

Our next step, we decided, was to explore our island. Since we had no idea of what dangers we might have to face, we cut two large clubs off a tree and Jack armed himself with the axe. We set off.

To begin with we followed the beach till we came to the entrance of a valley, through which flowed a little river. Here we turned our backs on the sea and struck inland.

At the head of the valley, about two miles off, stood a small mountain, all covered with trees except for a spot near the left shoulder, where we could see a bare and rocky cliff.

We reached the foot of the mountain and were passing through a grove of banana trees, when we were startled by a strange pattering and a rumbling sound.

We stopped short.

"What's that?" Peterkin cried.

Jack held his axe tight in his right hand and with the other pushed aside the broad leaves.

"I can't see anything—" he began.

The rumbling sound came again, louder than before. We stared all round, a little wild-eyed, expecting to see some gigantic animal bounding towards us. Then the pattering noise came again, much closer at hand this time. There was a fearful crash among the bushes, and a second later an enormous rock came hurtling through the undergrowth in a cloud of dust and small stones. It flew close past the spot where we stood, flattening the bushes and young trees in its path.

"Gosh! Is that all?" gasped Peterkin, wiping the sweat from his forehead. "I thought it was all the wild men in the South Sea Islands coming at us in one grand charge— and it was just a stone tumbling down the mountainside."

"If that stone had come a few feet this way," said Jack grimly, "it would have been the end of all of us!"

This was true, and we felt very thankful for our escape. On looking at the spot more closely, we found that it lay right under the high cliff that we had seen. It was clear

that stones had tumbled from it before as they were strewn all around on the ground.

We moved forward again, having made up our minds to keep clear of the place in future.

In a matter of minutes we were clambering up the steep sides of the mountain. We saw, when we reached its top, that it was not the highest point of the island, but that another mountain lay beyond, and between the two was a wide valley full of tall trees. We pushed on down the hill-side, crossed the valley, and began to climb the second mountain.

We were not far from the top when we had our second shock of the day. That was when Jack, who was in the lead, came to a sudden halt and gave an exclamation of surprise.

"Look at that!" he cried, and pointed at the stump of a tree.

I stared and for a moment I was puzzled. Then I saw what he meant. The tree had been cut down with an axe. We were not the first to walk upon this beautiful isle!

Chapter Four

The Shark

We moved closer to the tree-stump and looked at it closely. There could be no doubt at all that it had been cut by the hand of man. The wood was all decayed and partly covered with moss, so that it must have been done a long time before.

We stared at it in silence for a few seconds.

"Perhaps a ship put in here for wood," said Peterkin.

Jack shook his head.

"That's not the answer," he said. "The crew of a ship would cut any wood they wanted close to the shore. This was a large tree—and it stood near the top of the mountain." He frowned and scratched at the stump with his axe. "I can't understand it," he went on. "It must be the work of savages—but wait a moment! What's this?"

He bent over the stump as he spoke and began to scrape more carefully. As the moss fell away, I saw three distinct marks, as if someone had carved his initials upon the trunk. They looked like J. S., but were so broken up that we could not be sure what they were.

It was all very puzzling and we spent a long time wondering how the marks had got there. Then, as the day was wearing on, we began climbing once more.

From the top of the mountain we could see our kingdom

laid out like a map beneath us, with all its woods and valleys, plains and sparkling streams. It was roughly circular in shape and about ten miles across, the whole island belted by a beach of pure white sand, on which washed the gentle ripples of the lagoon. Out at sea lay about a dozen other islands at various distances from half a mile to ten miles. All of them, as far as we could tell, were smaller than ours and much lower on the sea.

As the day was now well on we turned back the way we had come. We had not gone far when once more we found traces of man. These were a pole or staff, and one or two blocks of wood which had been squared with an axe. All were very much decayed and must have lain untouched for years. We also found the prints of some four-footed animal, but could not tell whether they were old or new.

We sat up late that night, talking our heads off and trying to solve the riddle of the felled tree. At last, however, we made up our minds that the island must be uninhabited, and went to bed.

For several days after we did not go far from our camp. We bathed a lot, talked a great deal, and, among other useful things, Jack turned about three inches of the hoop-iron into a fine sharp knife. First he beat it quite flat with the axe. Then he made a rough handle, tied the hoop-iron to it with our piece of cord, and ground the iron to an edge on a piece of hard sandstone. When the blade was finished, he used it to shape a better handle.

Peterkin then tried using the cord as a fishing-line. To the end of it he tied a piece of oyster; this the fish were

allowed to swallow, and then they were pulled ashore. As the line was very short, however, and we had no boat, the fish we caught were all very small.

One day Peterkin came up from the beach, where he had been fishing, and said:

"Jack, I think we ought to have a shot at making a boat. I want to go fishing in deeper water."

Jack thought about it for a minute or two.

"I'll tell you what we could do," he said at last. "We'll fell a large tree and launch the trunk of it in the water. We could all float on that."

It seemed to be a good idea. We found a tree that grew close to the water's edge, and Jack set to work with the axe. Within half an hour it came crashing down.

"Now for it!" he cried. "Off with its head!"

While he was lopping off the branches, Peterkin and I shaped two rough paddles, and then the three of us rolled the log into the lagoon.

Once it was well afloat, we climbed aboard. This was easy to do; but after seating ourselves astride the log we found that it rolled round and plunged us into the water. It took an hour's practice for us to become expert enough to keep our balance pretty steadily.

We decided to go deep-sea fishing.

Peterkin baited his line with a whole oyster. Then we paddled out and dropped the line into deep water.

After a minute or two Peterkin gave an excited shout.

"There's a big fellow down there. Gosh! He's swallowed the bait! What a whacker!"

I could see that the fish was a big one. As it came struggling to the surface we all leaned forward to see it—and overturned the log. Peterkin threw his arms round the neck of the fish, and in another instant we were all floundering in the water.

We rose to the surface like three drowned rats and seized hold of the log. One by one we climbed back on to it and sat more warily while Peterkin secured the fish and rebaited the line. Then he dropped it in again.

Suddenly there was a ripple on the sea, only a few yards from us. Peter shouted for us to paddle in that direction. As I swung up my paddle I heard Jack give a shout that froze the blood in my veins.

"Peterkin, pull in the line! Grab your paddle, quick!— It's a shark!"

A second later I saw a sharp fin appear above the surface of the water and cut through it towards the log.

Chapter Five

A Cry in the Night

We were all filled with horror. We sat with our legs dangling in the water and dared not pull them out for fear of unsettling the log.

Peterkin pulled in the line and grabbed his paddle. We began paddling frantically for the shore, while the shark, which had veered off a little, swam round and round us with its sharp fin sticking out of the water. I saw suddenly, with a thrill of fear, that it was moving closer as if to attack.

Jack shouted.

"Look out! He's coming!"

I stared at the water with panic-stricken eyes and saw the long sleek body dive close under us, and then the white of the belly as the shark turned half over on his side.

"Splash with your paddles!" Jack cried, and we all beat at the water to kick up a great splashing and foaming.

For a moment the shark was frightened off. It went back to circling around us.

"Throw him that fish, Peterkin!" cried Jack. "We'll make the shore yet, if we can keep him off for a few minutes."

Peterkin threw the fish, then plied his paddle once more with all his might.

I saw the fish touch the water and had a glimpse of the

white breast as the shark rose; then the snout appeared with its wide jaws and its double row of teeth. The fish was gone, and the shark sank back out of sight. We paddled furiously for the shore and then the fin appeared again and began circling close to us.

"Stop paddling," Jack ordered suddenly. "Do as I tell you—and do it *quickly*. Do your best to balance the log, and don't look out for the shark. Leave him to me!"

Peterkin and I did as we were ordered. For a few seconds, that seemed like long minutes to my mind, we sat in silence; but I could not help looking back . . .

I saw Jack, sitting like a statue, his paddle raised, his lips pressed tightly together, and his eyes glaring down into the water. I also saw the shark, very close, darting towards Jack's foot. My heart was in my throat. I gave a cry. The shark rose, and I saw Jack whip his leg out of the water and throw it over the log. The shark's snout rubbed against the log, and it showed its hideous jaws. A second later Jack thrust hard down with the paddle and plunged it into the monster's throat. As he did so he rose to his feet so that the log was rolled right over and the three of us plunged into the water. We rose, spluttering and gasping.

"Get ashore!" yelled Jack. "Peterkin, grab my collar and kick out like mad!"

Peterkin did as he was told, and Jack struck out with such force that he cut through the water like a boat. I went after him and a minute later we were all in shallow water.

We flopped down on to the sand, worn out by our terrible adventure, and much shaken by the thought that we

had run the same danger while bathing in the lagoon. It was clear that we had to do something about that.

At last we thought of searching for a large pool among the rocks, where the water would be deep enough for diving, yet so surrounded by rocks that no shark could get at us. And such a pool we found, not ten minutes' walk from our camp: a small, deep bay with a narrow, shallow entrance that no fish as large as a shark could get through.

But there could be no more deep-sea fishing until we had made a raft or a boat . . .

A few days later we made up our minds to do something we had often talked about—to travel right round the island. Before we set out, however, Jack suggested that we should arm ourselves in some way.

"It would be a good idea to make bows and arrows," he said, "and have a shot at getting some animal food. And there's another thing—if we had some candles we could work at night. Now, I know that there's a certain nut that grows in the South Sea that the natives call the candlenut. I know all about it and how to prepare it for burning."

"Then why don't you do it?" asked Peterkin.

"Because," Jack answered, "I've not yet seen the tree on which it grows."

"What are the nuts like?" I asked.

"They're about the size of a walnut; and I think the leaves are white."

Peterkin gave a start.

"I saw a tree like that today," he said eagerly. "It's only about half a mile away."

Jack rose and seized his axe.

"Lead me to it," he ordered.

In a few minutes we were pushing through the underwood of the forest, led by Peterkin.

We soon found the tree. Its leaves were silvery white, and we filled our pockets with the nuts.

"Now, Peterkin," said Jack when we had done that, "just climb that coconut tree and cut me one of the long branches."

Peterkin shinned up the tree and threw down a branch about fifteen feet long, with a number of narrow, pointed leaflets ranged down both sides. There was also something like coarse brown cotton cloth wrapped round the end of the stalk where it had been cut from the tree. This strange piece of cloth we stripped off. It was about two feet long by a foot broad, and we carried it home with us as a great prize.

Jack then took one of the leaflets and cut out the central spine or stalk. Having made a small fire, he baked the nuts slightly, and then peeled off the husks. After that Jack bored a hole in them with the point of our pencil-case. I watched him string the nuts on the coconut spine and then, to my amazement, when he put a light to the topmost nut I saw it begin to burn with a clear, bright flame.

"So far, so good," said Jack, blowing out our candle, "but the sun will be down in an hour, so we've no time to lose. I'm going to cut a young tree to make a bow and you'd better find some strong sticks for clubs. We'll set to work on them after dark."

We did as we were told and, when darkness came down, we lit a candle inside the camp, sat down on our leafy beds, and set to work.

Jack started chipping at the piece of wood he had brought in with him, while Peterkin tried to fit a small, sharp piece of the hoop-iron to the end of a long pole.

"What's that for?" I asked.

"I'm making a spear instead of a club," Peterkin answered.

"Good idea," I said. "I think I'll change my mind too. I'm going to make a sling out of this piece of cloth. I used to be pretty handy with a sling."

For some time we worked in silence. At last Peterkin looked up.

"Jack," he said, "may I have a strip of your handkerchief to tie on my spearhead? It's pretty well torn up already, and—"

He stopped dead and his eyes widened. Over the island there rang out a strange and horrible cry that seemed to come from the sea.

Chapter Six
The Water-spouts

I felt a chill run up my back. The sound came again, loud and clear on the still night air—a long and hideous cry. We all started to our feet, and stared out across the sea. The moon had risen and we could see the islands in and beyond the lagoon, but there was nothing stirring anywhere. The sound died away while we were gazing at the sea.

"What is it?" asked Peterkin, in a low, frightened whisper.

"I've heard it before," said Jack, "but never as loud as that. I thought I might have imagined it, so I said nothing to you."

We listened for a long time, but the sound was not made again. We sat down and started work once more, all of us a little uneasy.

There was a silence.

"Ralph, do you believe in ghosts?" asked Peterkin at last.

I shook my head.

"No," I said. "I don't!"

"What about you, Jack?"

"I don't either. I don't know what made that sound, but I'll find out before long. Now, I've finished my bow and arrows, so if you're ready, we'd better get to sleep."

By this time Peterkin had thinned down his spear and tied an iron point to the end of it, I had made a sling from plaited strips of the coconut cloth, and Jack had made a strong bow, nearly five feet long, with several arrows that he'd feathered from plumes dropped by birds.

So it was that we were all well armed when we set out on our expedition the next morning. The day was still and peaceful, its silence broken only by the little twitter of birds among the bushes and the distant boom of the surf upon the reef.

Half a mile's walk took us round a bend in the land which shut our camp from view, and for some time we strode on without speaking, till we reached the mouth of a valley that we had not explored before. We were about to turn into it when Peterkin stopped and pointed along the shore.

"What's that?" he said.

As he spoke, I saw a white column of something like steam or spray shoot up above the rocks. It hung there for a moment and then disappeared. The odd thing was that it was about fifty yards inland, among rocks that stretched across the sandy beach to the sea. As we stood gaping, a second column flew up for a few seconds—and disappeared.

Jack started forward.

"Come on," he said. "Let's see what it is."

We reached the spot in a couple of minutes. The rocks were high and steep and damp with the falling of spray. Here and there were holes in the ground. We looked round, puzzled, as there came a low, rumbling sound near us. It

grew into a gurgling and hissing that seemed to come from under our feet and a moment later a thick spout of water burst from a hole in the rock only a few feet off. We sprang to one side, but not before a cloud of spray had drenched us to the skin.

Peterkin, who had been well clear, gave a roar of laughter. "Mind your eye!" he shouted. "There goes another!"

At the same instant a spout shot from another hole and drenched us even more.

Peterkin was now doubled up with laughter, but suddenly there came a loud hiss and a fierce spout of water burst under his legs, threw him off his feet, drenched him in spray, and landed him in a clump of tangled bushes.

It was our turn to laugh; then the three of us ran from the spot before we were caught again.

We looked at our wet and dripping clothes.

"We'll have to make a fire and dry them," said Jack.

I carried the burning-glass in my pocket, and in a few minutes we had a fire going and our clothes hanging up before it. While they were drying we walked down to the beach and we soon found out that these curious spoutings took place after the fill of a wave. We decided that there must be an underground channel in the rocks, that the water was driven into it, and that, having no way of escape except through the holes, it was forced up through them.

We moved along the cliff a bit. Suddenly Jack gave a shout. I ran to the overhanging ledge of rock from which he was looking down into the sea.

"What's that in the water?" he asked. "Is it a shark?"

Down in the water I could see a faint, pale object of a greenish colour, which seemed to be moving slightly

"It's a fish of some sort," I said.

Jack turned and yelled for Peterkin.

"Bring your spear," he bawled.

Peterkin did so but the spear was too short for us to reach the object with it, so Jack raised it, drove it down into the water, and let go his hold. He must have missed. When the spear rose again, there was the pale green object in the same spot, slowly moving its tail.

We took it in turn to plunge the spear into the water again and again, but we could neither hit the thing nor drive it away. We continued our journey without discovering what it was.

As we moved on along the little valley we were lucky enough to find a large supply of yams, and another root like a potato. We stuffed our pockets with them, planning to eat them for our supper.

This valley took us into another, larger, one, in which we found a clump of chestnuts growing on the bank of a stream. Jack struck his axe into one with all his force and split off a large slice of wood, to satisfy himself that we could cut short planks if we needed them at a later date.

The sun was sinking as we wended our way back towards the shore. We wanted to camp near the beach because the mosquitoes were so troublesome in the forest. As we went, we were startled by a loud, whistling noise above our heads and saw a flock of wild-ducks making for the coast. We

watched them, saw where they came down, and followed after them until we reached a most lovely blue lake about two hundred yards long, from which rose a cloud of ducks and water-hens as we appeared.

Jack suggested that he and I should go a little out of our way to see if we could shoot one of the ducks, while Peterkin went on to the shore and built a fire.

We saw nothing more of the ducks though we searched for half an hour, and we were about to start back when we were faced with one of the strangest sights we had yet seen on the island.

It was on the edge of a clearing. About ten yards in front of us grew a huge tree, with clusters of bright yellow fruit hanging from its branches. Under the tree lay at least twenty hogs of all ages and sizes, all fast asleep.

We watched them for a second, then Jack put a hand on my arm.

"Put a stone in your sling," he whispered, "and let fly at that big fellow with his back to you. I'll try to put an arrow in one of the others. Don't miss if you can help it, for we badly need the meat."

I slung my stone with such a good aim that it smacked against the hog's flank as if against a drum. The animal started to its feet with a squeal of surprise, and scampered away through the trees. At the same instant Jack's bow twanged and an arrow pinned one of the little pigs to the ground by its ear.

"He's getting away," Jack yelled, and darted forward with uplifted axe.

The little pig gave a loud squeal, tore the arrow from the ground, and ran away with it, along with the whole drove. We went crashing through the bushes after them, but were unable to catch them.

"No pork supper tonight," said Jack ruefully. "We'd better hurry up and look for Peterkin."

We worked our way back towards the shore, where we found a fire burning, but no sign of Peterkin at all. Jack gave a shout. As if in answer, we heard a distant shriek, followed by a chorus of squeals from the hogs.

"I believe Peterkin's run into them," I said excitedly.

There was a great deal of squealing, and then a distant shout. Along the beach we saw Peterkin walking towards us with a little pig stuck on the end of his long spear.

"Peterkin, you're the best shot among us," said Jack, giving him a slap on the shoulder.

Peterkin held out the pig and pointed to its ear.

"Do you see that hole?" he said. "And do you know this arrow, eh? You hit him first. But never mind that. I'm hungry! Let's get supper going."

It took us some time, however, to make up our minds how to cook the pig. We had never cut one up before, and we did not know how to begin. In the end, we cut off the legs with the axe, along with a large part of the flesh, made some deep gashes in them, thrust a sharp-pointed stick through each, and stuck them up before the blaze to roast. While they were cooking, we scraped a hole in the sand and ashes under the fire, put in the vegetables we had found, and covered them up.

The meal, when cooked, seemed to taste better than anything we had ever eaten before. We had our fill, then lay down to sleep upon a couch of branches under an overhanging shelf of rock. We slept soundly and well that night—happily unaware of the gruesome discovery that we were to make the next day.

Chapter Seven

The Hut

The sun was already high when we awoke. We all felt strong and well and made a good breakfast of cold pork and fruit.

We set out, but had not gone more than a mile or so, when, as we turned a point that showed us a new and beautiful cluster of islands beyond the reef, we heard the appalling cry that had so alarmed us a few nights before.

We stood stockstill. The sound came again, louder than before.

"It's coming from one of those islands," said Jack.

We all peered towards the islands. And then I jumped with surprise. On the shore of the largest I could see some curious objects moving. At that distance they looked like an army of soldiers, marching in lines and squares. Even as we stared, that dreadful cry came again across the water.

And then Jack laughed.

"They're penguins," he said. "It's their cry we've been hearing. When we've built our boat we'll go over and have a look at them."

We went on our way, much lighter at heart for having solved the mystery of the ghostly cry.

It was that afternoon that we found the footprints of a small animal, which were something like those of a dog.

There were a lot of them, running off into the woods along a beaten track which seemed too wide to have been made by the animal itself. We followed them and had gone some way when we came upon an open space and heard a faint cry. We all started in surprise. On the track before us stood a small black animal.

"It's a wildcat!" cried Jack, and let fly with an arrow.

He missed. The arrow struck the earth about two feet to one side. The wildcat, to our surprise, did not bolt away, but walked slowly towards the arrow and sniffed at it.

"It's tame!" cried Peterkin.

"I think it's blind," I said. "Look, it keeps walking into branches as it moves along. It must be very old."

We hurried towards it. It did not hear our footsteps until we were right up to it, seeming deaf as well as blind. It gave a hoarse mew.

Peterkin went over and patted its head.

"Poor old thing!" he said gently. "Poor pussy; chee, chee, chee; puss, puss, puss; cheetie pussy!"

The cat stood still and let him stroke it, then rubbed itself against his legs, purring loudly all the time. Peterkin lifted it in his arms.

"It's no more a wildcat than I am," he said. "Poor pussy!"

We watched in amazement as the cat rubbed its head against Peterkin's cheek, and mewed and purred to show its pleasure. It was quite clear that the poor animal had known man before, and was showing its joy at meeting human beings.

At last we decided to follow the track, and went on with

Peterkin carrying the cat. After fifty yards or so the track turned to the right and wandered for a short space along the banks of a stream. We were quite startled when we came to a spot where there must once have been a crude bridge, the stones of which were now scattered in the stream. We moved on, more expectant now, until, under the shelter of some bread-fruit trees, we came upon a small hut.

We stopped and stood for a long time in silent wonder. There was a deep and melancholy stillness about the place, a kind of sadness about this broken, lonely hut so far from the usual dwellings of man. It was roughly twelve feet long and seven or eight feet high. It had one opening for a window and the door was very low. The roof was of coconut and plantain leaves. Most of it was in a state of decay.

We stood and talked in whispers before any of us dared go near the place. Then Jack stole forward and tried to peer in through the window. He could see nothing in the deep shadow of the trees, so we lifted the rusty iron latch and pushed the door open. It gave an eerie creak as it swung back. We entered and gazed around us.

As my eyes grew used to the dim light I made out a wooden stool standing beside a roughly hewn table, on which stood an iron pot. Then my gaze moved on and my heart gave a sudden, frightened leap. In the corner farthest from the door was a low bedstead, and on it lay the skeleton of a man.

Chapter Eight
The Diamond Cave

For long, long moments we stood staring in the awful stillness of the place; then Jack stepped forward to the bed and we followed him with beating hearts.

There were two skeletons, I saw, lying in a little heap of dust. One was that of a man, and the other that of a dog, its head resting on its master's chest. We searched the hut for some clue to the identity of this poor man, but we found nothing that helped at all.

We talked about him in whispers. I said that he must have been a shipwrecked sailor, cast away with only his cat and dog for company. There seemed to be no other answer.

Then came a sudden exclamation from Peterkin, who was turning over a heap of broken wood and rubbish that lay in a corner.

"Look here! These should be useful."

"What are they?" asked Jack, hastening across the room.

"An old pistol and an axe," Peterkin replied.

"We might as well take them," said Jack quietly, "though the gun won't be any use without powder."

We took these things and the iron pot with us. Peter lifted the cat and we left the hut. As we did so, Jack stumbled heavily against the doorpost, which was so decayed that it

broke across, and the whole hut seemed ready to tumble about our ears. This put it into our heads that we might as well pull it down and let it form a grave for the skeletons.

Jack swung his axe at the other doorpost and brought the whole hut in ruins to the ground. We continued our journey, though we did not recover our good spirits till we got back to our camp, late on the next day.

For several weeks after this we were busy cutting and shaping wood with which to make a boat. And then one morning, after we had bathed and eaten, Peterkin rose and said:

"I could do with a rest. I'm tired of cutting and hammering. Let's do something different today."

"All right," said Jack. "What shall we do?"

I was the first to answer.

"Do you remember the green thing we saw in the water close to the water-spouts? Let's see if it's still there."

The others readily agreed, and we took up our weapons and set out. When we reached the place and gazed down into the sea, there was the same pale green object moving its tail to and fro in the water.

"Well, this beats everything!" said Peterkin. "Let's have another shot at moving it with my spear."

A second later his spear flashed down into the water. Down it went, straight into the centre of the green object, passed right through it, and came up again. Below us the mysterious tail still moved quietly to and fro.

We looked at each other.

"I don't think it's alive at all," said Jack. "I think it's merely a light. Anyway, as long as it isn't a shark there's no reason

why we shouldn't dive down to it. I'm going to have a look."

He stripped off his clothes, joined his hands above his head, and plunged into the sea. For a second or so he was hidden by the spray of his dive; then the water became still and we saw him swimming far down towards the green object.

And then he vanished!

We held our breath and waited for him to reappear. A minute passed, two, three—and still he did not come. We waited a little longer, and then a panic took hold of me. Peterkin started to his feet, his face deadly pale.

"Ralph!" he said hoarsely. "He needs help. Dive for him, Ralph."

I was already on my feet. In a moment I was poised on the edge of the rocks, and was on the point of diving when I saw something black shooting up through the water. Another second and Jack's head rose to the surface. He gave a shout and shook the spray from his hair; then I put out an arm and helped him clamber up to the ledge.

He sank down, panting for breath.

"Jack," cried Peterkin, and there were tears in his eyes, "where were you?"

Jack grinned.

"Lads," he said, "that green object is a stream of light that comes from a cave in the rocks underneath us. I swam right into it, saw a faint light above me, darted up, and found my head out of water. At first I couldn't see much, it was so dark; but when my eyes got used to the light, I

found that I was in a big cave. I could see part of the walls and the roof. I had a good look round; then I thought that you two might be getting a bit worried, so I shot back up again."

This was enough to make me want to see the cave, but Jack told me to wait for a minute or two because he wanted to take down a torch, and set fire to it in the cave.

I waited while he cut some strips of inflammable bark off a tree, and cemented them together with a kind of gum from another tree. When this was ready, he wrapped it up in several pieces of the coconut cloth; then he took a small piece of the tinder from the old pistol we had found, rolled up some dry grass, and made another bundle protected by the cloth.

At last we were ready. We walked to the edge of the rocks, Jack carrying one bundle and I the other. Peterkin, who could not dive, watched us with a mournful face.

"Don't worry about us, Peterkin," said Jack. "We may not be back for half an hour."

The next moment we sprang from the rock together.

It was easy to find the entrance to the cave. I watched Jack swim through, then went straight after him. There was light above me. I came up to the surface and trod water, holding my bundle above my head. As soon as our eyes were used to the faint light, we swam to a shelf of rock and clambered out on to it.

Inside five minutes our torch flared into life. I gazed all round me, struck dumb by the wonders it showed.

The whole place flashed and gleamed. Its roof was made

of coral, and from it hung glistening icicles that were really a sort of limestone. As we walked forward along the ledge we saw that the floor was made of the same stuff; its surface all rippled like water when ruffled by the wind.

In the walls on either hand were several openings that seemed to lead off into other caves, but these we did not explore. We moved far into the big cavern, without reaching the end of it. Its walls and roof sparkled in the glare of the torch, and threw back gleams and flashes just as if they were covered with precious stones.

We turned back when the torch began to burn down. What was left of it we placed in a dry spot. Then we plunged back off the ledge, dived through the entrance, and shot up to the surface.

As we dressed and walked home we tried to tell Peterkin all about the wonders of our Diamond Cave, little guessing then how much use it would prove to be in a moment of urgent danger . . .

Chapter Nine

Penguin Island

Our boat, at last, was finished.

It looked a clumsy thing, but it did our hearts good to see it. Its planks were of chestnut, and its keel made from a small tree which had a branch growing at the proper angle about ten feet up its stem. The planks were nailed to the keel with wooden pegs, driven hard through holes that we had bored through the timber with a length of red-hot hoop-iron. The oars we blocked out roughly with the axe; then we smoothed them down with the knife.

It was a bright clear morning when we first launched the boat upon the lagoon. The sea was like a sheet of glass, and in its depths shone the brilliant corals. We rowed and fished for an hour or two and found that the boat handled surprisingly well.

"The next thing," said Jack, "is to make a mast and sail. I'll see to the mast and you two can collect coconut cloth for the sail. Let's get to work."

In three days we had set up the mast and sail. The sail was made of a number of oblong pieces of cloth that we had sewn together with our needle. It worked perfectly, and we cruised about over the lagoon, fishing, and watching for hours the brightly coloured fish that swam among the corals and seaweed.

Soon after we'd finished the boat, we were sitting on the rocks at Spouting Cliff, and talking about a sail we planned to make to Penguin Island, on the very next day. As we sat there I noticed a dark line, like a low cloud or fogbank, on the seaward horizon. The day was fine, though cloudy, and the seas breaking on the reef were no higher than usual. We thought a storm might be brewing, and kept our eyes on that strange dark line that seemed to draw nearer without spreading up over the sky. It moved swiftly, but there was no sound till it reached an island out at sea. At its touch a cloud of white foam burst in spray that rose high in the air. There was a loud roar and then, for the first time, we realized that we were calmly gazing at a monster wave, sweeping in towards us.

We sprang to our feet.

"Run!" Jack shouted. "Quickly—get on high ground!"

We raced towards a hill that rose behind us, and scrambled to its summit. There we turned, wide-eyed and panting, in time to see the great wave strike the reef.

It burst right over with a roar like thunder, then rolled on towards the shore. Its great crest seemed to rear higher and higher, and then, with a crash that shook the solid rocks, it fell. In that moment it seemed as if all the earth had been blown up with water. We were stunned and confused by the shock, and blinded by flying spray. The wave swept across the beach and dashed into the woods, smashing down trees and bushes in its headlong course.

As soon as the water had flowed back, we tore down the hill, afraid that our camp might have been swept away,

and that our boat, which we had pulled up on to the beach, might have been utterly destroyed. The camp, we found, was safe, for the wave had not flowed that far, though there were torn-up bushes and tangled heaps of seaweed only a few feet from the entrance.

Our next thought was for the boat. We hurried down to the beach and found that it was gone.

We started towards the woods, our eyes searching everywhere for some sign of the missing boat. Then Peterkin gave a shout.

"Jack! What sort of fruit is that growing on top of that bush there?"

We stared and saw our boat perched upside-down on the top of a large bush. Luckily it was not damaged in any way, though it was hard work to get it out of the bush and down to the sea again.

The weather next morning was so good, and the sea so quiet, that we made up our minds to sail across to Penguin Island as we had planned. We rowed over the lagoon towards the outlet in the reef, and slipped between the two green islets that guarded the entrance. We shipped some water in the surf, but then found ourselves floating smoothly enough on a long oily swell.

We had about twenty miles to go. Rowing was hard work, but after we had covered a mile or two a breeze got up, so we spread our sail and flew merrily over the waves.

As we drew close to the island, we were much amused by the antics of the penguins as they strutted to and fro, or marched in ranks like soldiers.

There were thousands of them on the rock, and we pulled in and lay there for more than an hour watching the habits of these curious birds.

It was late afternoon when we turned away from the island. We had made up our minds to camp for the night on another smaller island on which we could see a few coconut trees growing, about two miles off.

The sky darkened as we went. Before we were half-way the breeze had freshened until it was blowing a gale, and the waves began to rise against the boat so that she took in water, and it was all we could do to keep afloat.

We at last realized that we could never make the island. Jack put the boat around and called for the sail to be hoisted, to run back to Penguin Island.

"If we can get there, we'll at least have shelter," he said.

Even as he spoke the wind shifted and began to blow so much against us that it was clear that it would not be easy to beat up for the island.

"You'll have to take in sail," Jack shouted above the wind.

Peterkin and I hurried to obey. We had the sail down in a moment but were then struck by a sudden squall that left the boat half full of water. I started baling, while Peterkin again raised a corner of the sail.

Several minutes passed. When I had finished baling, I sat up and stared around me. In that moment the awful truth dawned upon me. It would be impossible for us to reach Penguin Island. Our small and leaky boat was being swept out into the ocean.

Chapter Ten
Cannibals

I was scared stiff.

At any moment one of the huge waves which curled over in masses of foam might easily swallow up the boat. Water kept washing over the sides and I had to keep on baling alone, for Jack dared not leave the helm nor Peterkin the sail.

Several minutes passed. Then came a shout from Jack.

"Look—a rock—or an island—straight ahead!"

Hope sprang up inside me. I baled furiously, then sat up and looked ahead. I had not seen the island before because of the dark clouds that filled the sky, and the blinding spray that flew into my eyes.

The island was bare of trees—a sea-pounded stretch of coral sand that rose only two or three feet out of the water. And my heart sank again when I saw that there was not a spot where we could thrust our little boat without its being dashed to pieces.

"Show a bit more sail," Jack ordered, as we went sweeping past the weather side of the rock with fearful speed it seemed we would be swept passed the island.

The extra bit of sail was enough to lay the boat right over. It creaked so loudly that I felt sure it would overturn, but somehow Jack managed to steer us sharply round to

the leeward side of the rock, where the water seemed almost calm and the force of the wind was broken.

"Out with the oars!" Jack cried.

We obeyed at once. Two or three good strong pulls on the oars and we were floating in a little creek so narrow that it would barely admit the boat. We leaped ashore and made our craft fast to the rocks. Even then our plight was far from happy. We had brought plenty of food with us, but we were drenched to the skin, the attacking sea was foaming all round us, and the spray flew over our heads. At the upper end of the creek, however, was a small hollow in the rock, which would give us some shelter against the sea and wind.

We landed our provisions, wrung the water out of our clothing, spread our sail for a carpet, and ate a cold meal. By then we were feeling more cheerful, but as night drew on our spirits sank again.

We lay there in the darkness, unable to see the rock, and stunned by the fury of the storm. From time to time the spray blew into our faces and the sea, in its mad boiling, washed up into our little creek until it reached our feet. Flashes of lightning shone with a ghastly glare through the watery curtains around us and gave an added horror to the scene, while crashing peals of thunder seemed to split the skies in two.

Again and again we fancied that the solid rock was giving way, and in our agony we clung to the bare ground, expecting every second to be whirled away into the black, howling sea.

Somehow the hours dragged by, and at last we saw the gleam of dawn breaking through the mists. This, however, was not the end of our ordeal . . .

For three days and nights we were chained to that rock, and all the time the storm raged with unabated fury. Then, on the morning of the fourth day, the wind dropped. By the middle of the morning the sea was dead calm and the sun was shining.

It was with light hearts that we launched our boat once more and pulled away for Coral Island. The breeze rose an hour later, but we did not reach the outer reef till dusk. The moon and stars were shining in the sky when we came to our camp and found the poor old black cat curled up asleep inside.

For many months after we lived happily enough. Sometimes we went fishing in the lagoon, sometimes we hunted in the woods, and often we climbed to the mountain-top to look for passing ships.

The weather was so fine, our island so beautiful, that it all seemed like a never-ending summer—until there happened something that was alarming and horrible.

It was when we were sitting on the rocks at Spouting Cliff one day that I noticed the two dark objects that had appeared on the horizon.

We stared at them for a long time.

"They're coming closer," I said.

"I think they're whales," said Peterkin, shading his eyes with his hands. "No, wait—can they be *boats*, Jack?"

Jack gazed out across the sea.

"They *are* boats," he said at last.

I felt my heart begin to pound with excitement.

We were all on our feet now, staring out across the sunlit sea. Suddenly Jack gave a start.

"They're canoes," he said. "They may be war-canoes. I don't like the look of this. We mustn't forget that a lot of the natives of these islands are fierce cannibals. We'd better hide until we know what to make of them. Come on— behind the rocks!"

A minute later we lay hidden, each one of us with a thick club in his hand and his eyes on the approaching canoes.

It was soon clear that one was chasing the other. The one in the lead held about forty people, among them a few women and children. The canoe which pursued them held only men, who were paddling with all their might. It looked like a war-canoe.

The first canoe made for the shore almost right below us. The paddles flashed in and out of the water and threw up a shower of spray. From where I lay I could see the eyes of the paddlers glistening in the sunlight. As the canoe grounded on the sand, the whole party sprang to the shore. Three women and a girl rushed away into the woods, while the men crowded to the water's edge, waving spears and clubs as if to threaten the approaching enemy.

The second canoe came on unchecked. It struck the beach, and its savage crew leaped into the water and rushed to the attack.

The attackers were led by a tall, strong chief whose hair was frizzed out all round his head. It was light yellow in

colour and I could only think that it must have been dyed. He was tattooed from head to foot, his whole body smeared and streaked with red and white paint.

The battle that followed was frightful to watch. Most of the men wielded great clubs, with which they dashed out each other's brains.

As they leaped and bounded and pounced for the kill, they looked more like devils than human beings. I felt my heart grow sick within me at the awful sights I saw.

Suddenly the yellow-haired chief was attacked by a man as big and strong as himself. The two fought like demons, and then in an instant Yellow Hair tripped and crashed down to the ground. His enemy sprang forward, club upraised, but before he could strike he, too, was felled to the ground by a stone from the hand of one who had seen his chief's danger.

That was the turning point. The savages who had landed first turned and fled towards the woods, but not one of them escaped. All were overtaken and dragged to the ground. Fifteen were seized alive, tied hand and foot with cords, and thrown down upon the sand. Then they were left where they lay while their captors moved along the beach and began dressing their wounds and three or four of their number were sent running into the woods to search for the women we had seen come ashore.

Still we stayed behind our rock. I saw another of the savages go up into the woods and return with a great bundle of firewood. He crouched down upon the sand and soon had a big fire blazing on the beach. Yellow Hair gave a

shout, and two of his followers went over to the captives and began dragging one of them towards the fire.

A dreadful feeling of horror crept over me. I could see that these savages meant to burn their enemies. I gasped for breath and made to spring to my feet, but Jack grabbed hold of me and held me where I was. A second later one of the savages swung up his club to smash it down on the skull of his enemy. It was horrible. I turned away, and when I looked again Yellow Hair and his men were roasting something over the fire. I could guess what it was . . .

There came a scream from the woods. A minute later two of the savages came out of the woods, one dragging by the hair a woman who carried a baby in her arms, and the other struggling with the girl we had already seen.

Yellow Hair rose and walked towards the woman carring the baby. He put his hand upon the child. The woman wailed in fear and shrank away from him. He let out a wild laugh, tore the child from her arms, and threw it violently down upon the sands. The mother shrieked and crumpled in a faint.

I heard Jack moan.

The young girl was dragged forward, and Yellow Hair spoke to her. It seemed to me, by the way he pointed to the fire, that he was threatening her life.

A great hatred took hold of me.

"Peterkin," said Jack, in a hoarse whisper, "have you got your knife?"

"Yes," replied Peterkin in a strange voice.

I looked at him and saw that he was as white as death.

"Listen," said Jack between his teeth, "I want you to make a dash for the prisoners, and cut them loose. I'll keep the others busy. Go on, before it's too late."

He rose, his great club gripped in his hand. I heard him give a yell that rang like a death-shriek among the rocks. He went leaping towards the savages.

"Come on," cried Peterkin to me, and the two of us went darting across the sands towards the prisoners.

Chapter Eleven
The "Jolly Roger"

As I dropped beside the first of the bound men I looked over my shoulder and saw Jack rushing upon Yellow Hair, swinging his club.

The chief leaped back as quick as a cat, and at the same time aimed a blow at Jack. Now it was Jack's turn to spring aside, and then the two of them were fighting fiercely.

I tore at the cords that held the man's legs, while Peterkin went along the line slashing away with his knife. When I looked up again I saw Yellow Hair swing up his club. Then Jack darted in and struck the savage between the eyes with all his force. Yellow Hair fell forward and Jack, staggering, went down beneath the body of the chief.

The other savages yelled with fury. A dozen clubs were swung high, ready to crush Jack's skull, but the men hesitated for a moment, as if afraid to strike their chief.

That moment saved Jack's life. All the prisoners were free, and Peterkin and I led them across the sands, in a howling, shrieking mob, grabbing for stones and fallen clubs as we went.

A fierce hand-to-hand struggle followed. Seven of Yellow Hair's men went down beneath the clubs of the prisoners, who knew well enough that they were fighting for their lives. Our enemies were taken completely by surprise

and, I think, felt disheartened because of the fall of their chief. They were also overawed by the sweeping fury of Jack, who had no sooner shaken himself free of the chief's body than he rushed into the midst of them and struck down three men in as many blows.

Inside ten minutes all our opponents were either knocked down or made prisoners, bound hand and foot, and stretched out in a line upon the seashore.

We stood there, breathing hard, while the savages crowded around and jabbered away in their own tongue, which sounded so strange to our ears. I saw Jack take hold of the hand of the big man who was their chief (and who seemed to have recovered from the blow that had struck him down) and shake it warmly to show that we were friends. Then his eye fell upon the poor child that had been thrown upon the shore. Dropping the chief's hand, he hurried towards it and found that it was still alive. Its mother was lying upon the sand where she had fallen, and Jack carried the baby to her and laid its warm little cheek on hers. The effect was wonderful. The woman opened her eyes, felt the child, let out a scream of joy, and clasped the baby in her arms.

Jack turned away.

"Come on," he said to Peterkin and me. "Let's take them to the camp and hunt up some food."

Within half an hour all the savages were seated on the ground in front of our camp making a hearty meal of a cold roast pig, several ducks, some cold fish, and an un- limited supply of fruits.

As soon as we had eaten, we three, who now felt thoroughly exhausted, threw ourselves down on our beds and immediately fell fast asleep. Then the savages followed our example, and in a little while the whole camp was lost to the world.

The sun was up when I awoke, and the savages were already awake. We made a cold breakfast; then Jack signed to the savages to follow him down to the beach, where we had left the prisoners forgotten overnight.

They seemed none the worse of their night on the shore and they ate greedily of the food we gave them. Jack then began to dig a hole in the sand with one of the native paddles and after working at it for some time, he pointed to it and to the dead bodies that still lay stretched out upon the beach. The savages saw what he wanted, ran for their paddles, and inside an hour had dug a hole big enough to make a common grave.

The savages stayed with us for three days. During that time we made every effort to talk with them, but all we could learn was that their chief was named Tararo and that the young girl was called Avatea.

On the fourth day the whole party made ready to depart. We helped them to load their canoe with fruit and provisions, and to put the prisoners in it. Since we could not speak to say goodbye, we went through the ceremony of shaking hands. As soon as Tararo had done that, however, he took hold of Jack and rubbed noses with him. Then he did the same to Peterkin and me. I didn't think that was much fun.

Avatea was the last to take leave of us. Going up to Jack, she put out her flat little nose to be rubbed, then turned to me. I thought that was much more enjoyable . . .

Two hours later the canoe was out of sight and we were left with an odd feeling of sadness creeping round our hearts.

But the days passed by once more, and at last we began to think of the visit of the savages as if it had all been a terrible dream—until, that is, there happened something that was even more of a nightmare . . .

One afternoon Jack and I were sunning ourselves on the beach, while Peterkin was clambering about on a low cliff behind. Suddenly he gave a shout of the wildest excitement. We started up, wondering at the urgency in his voice.

"A sail!" he yelled. "Jack! Ralph! There's a ship coming this way!"

We clawed our way up the cliff to where he stood. There, right enough, was a schooner, outside the reef, but making for the island under a steady breeze.

We were mad with excitement.

The ship came on rapidly. In less than an hour she was close to the reef, where she rounded to and backed her topsails as if to survey the coast. We were all leaping and dancing and waving our arms, dreadfully afraid that we should not be seen. Then, to our great joy, we saw men beginning to lower a boat.

"They've seen us," yelled Peterkin. "They're coming ashore!"

And then several things happened all at once.

A flag was suddenly run up to the schooner's peak, and at the same time a little cloud of white smoke seemed to flower from her side, and an instant later a cannon-shot came crashing through the bushes and burst in atoms against the cliff, a few yards below the spot on which we stood.

For a moment we were frozen to the spot, filled with a sudden terror. The flag, we could see, was black, with a skull and cross-bones picked out upon it in white. It was the "Jolly Roger", the pirate flag feared upon all the seven seas.

"Pirates!" we said together.

The boat had now shot away from the schooner's side and was making for the entrance to the lagoon.

I looked at Jack.

"What are we going to do?" I asked.

"Hide," he said grimly. "We don't want to fall into *their* hands. Come on—quickly!"

He tore off into the woods and led us, by a winding path, to Spouting Cliff. Here he stopped, crept up behind a rock, and peered round its edge. I did the same and saw the boat, crowded with men, just running ashore. In another instant the crew had landed and were running up towards our camp.

A minute or so later we saw them hurrying back towards the boat, one of them swinging our poor cat round his head by its tail. When he reached the edge of the sea, he tossed it far out into the water, and moved towards his friends, roaring with laughter.

"You see what we can expect from them," said Jack bitterly. "If they decide to search the island, there's only one place we can go—down into the Diamond Cave."

Peterkin started.

"What about me?" he said. "I can't dive down there."

"We'll take you down," said Jack. "You'll just have to make up your mind to do it. There's nowhere else we can hide."

Peterkin gulped.

"All right," he said. "I'll do it. Come on!"

We crouched low and rushed towards the spot from which we always dived to the cave. Before we had gone far a hoarse shout came from the beach: the pirates had seen us. We sprang down to the ledge and Jack and I seized Peterkin by the arms.

"Keep quite still, Peterkin," said Jack, urgently. "Take a deep breath—and don't struggle. Let us take you."

Peterkin nodded. His face was set, and he looked ready to go through with anything.

"Right!" said Jack. "Now!"

As the pirates gained the foot of the rocks, which hid us for a moment from their view, we bent over the sea and plunged down together head foremost. Peterkin behaved like a hero.

He floated between us as stiff as a log of wood. We shot through the tunnel and rose into the cave more quickly than I had ever done it before.

We all took a long, deep breath and then scrambled out of the water. Jack groped around for the torch and tinder

which we always kept in the cave. Within two or three minutes the torch light was revealing to Peterkin the wonders he had never yet seen.

We decided that we should have to spend the night in the cave. At odd times Jack and I had carried coconuts and other fruits down to the cave, partly because we had an idea that we might be driven there by the savages one day and knew that if that happened we should be glad of a store of food. We wedged our torch in a crack in the rock and ate our supper, then sat and talked in whispers until the dim light that came through the entrance died away, and we knew that it was night. Then we put out our torch and settled down to sleep.

When I awoke I found it hard to remember where we were. We could see by the faint light that day had dawned, but we had no idea of the hour.

"One of us ought to dive out and have a look round," Jack suggested. "I'll go."

"No," I said. "You stay here. You've done enough for us already. Let me take a few risks for a change."

"All right," Jack agreed. "But keep a sharp look-out."

"Don't get caught," whispered Peterkin.

While the words were still sounding in my ears I plunged into the water, and swam out to the open air. I rose gently, and floated on my back, listening carefully. There was no sound but the twittering of the birds and the distant boom of the surf. Then I swam towards the ledge, pulled myself out, and climbed up the cliff a step at a time till I had a view of the shore.

I gave a cry of joy. As I looked out to sea, I saw the pirate schooner sailing away almost hull down on the horizon.

We were safe! I shouted again.

"There she goes! They've not caught us this time!"

Almost before I had finished speaking I heard a little movement behind me.

"I wouldn't be so sure of that," said a gruff voice. At the same moment a heavy hand clapped down on my shoulder and held it as if in a vice.

Chapter Twelve
The Schooner

My heart jumped into my throat. I jerked round, put up a desperate struggle to tear myself away, and received a slap on the side of the head for my pains. It left me half-dazed and stupid. Through tears of pain I looked up at the man who held me.

He seemed as tall as a tree. He was a white man, though his face was deeply bronzed by sun and wind. He had a beaky nose that was bent downwards in a bow, and his beard and moustache were lightly touched with grey. He wore the usual dress of a sailor, but there was a thick belt slung round his waist in which he had stuck a brace of pistols and a heavy cutlass.

He shook me.

"Don't try any tricks," he warned, and gave a shrill whistle.

It was answered at once, and a second or two later I saw the pirate long-boat sweep into sight around a jutting neck of land. It came rapidly towards us.

The man pushed me from him and drew one of his pistols. He waved it at me.

"Walk down to the beach," he said. "If you try to run away, I'll send a bullet after you!"

I obeyed. The long-boat was aground when I reached

the beach and a little knot of fierce-looking seamen stood on the sands and watched me approach.

"Get a fire going, one of you," ordered the man who had captured me.

A man sprang to obey. In a few minutes he had a fire burning, with clouds of thick smoke climbing into the air. Suddenly I heard the boom of a gun rolling over the sea and in a flash I saw how I had been tricked. The fire was a signal to recall the schooner, which had only pretended to put out to sea.

As the ship veered her head again, the pirates crowded round me—a tough-looking bunch with shaggy beards and scowling brows, all of them armed to the teeth. When they spoke to the man who had captured me they called him captain.

"Where are the other cubs?" cried one of the men, with an oath that made me shudder.

"I'll swear there were three of them."

"You hear what he says, whelp: where are the other dogs?" the captain demanded.

"I won't tell you," I answered in a low voice. The whole crew roared with laughter, while their captain cocked his pistol and said:

"I've no time to waste on you at the moment, but a taste of the thumb-screw will loosen your tongue, my lad." He turned to his men. "Put him in the boat," he ordered. "Look alive! The breeze is freshening."

A couple of the men grabbed hold of me, raised me shoulder high, swung me down the beach, and tossed me into

the bottom of their boat, where I struck my head on a seat and lay for some time half-stunned.

We were outside the reef and close alongside the schooner before I could think clearly once more. Someone swung a boot at me and a rough voice told me to jump aboard. I rose and clambered up the side. In a few minutes the boat was hoisted on deck, the ship's head put close to the wind, and the Coral Island dropping slowly astern as we beat up against a head sea. The crew were so busy working the ship that, for the moment, no one had any time for me. I leaned against the bulwarks, thinking of the friends I had left ashore, and a tear or two rolled slowly down my cheeks.

"So you're blubbering, are you?" said the deep voice of the captain. "Well, *there's* something to cry for," and he gave me a box on the ear that nearly felled me to the deck. "Clap a stopper on your eyes, and get below till I call you!"

As I moved to obey my eye fell on a small keg standing by the main-mast. Scrawled on its side in pencil was the word *gunpowder*. I saw, in an instant, that since we were beating up against the wind, anything floating in the sea would be driven on the reef encircling Coral Island. And I remembered that my friends had a pistol!

Without a second's hesitation, I grabbed up the keg and tossed it into the sea. There was a roar from the captain. He strode up to me, his hand raised to strike.

"You little rat!" he bawled. "What do you mean by that?"

"I've got some friends on that island," I answered. "They have a pistol, but no powder. Now, you can do what you like with me—"

The captain glared for a second and then, to my surprise, he smiled, turned on his heel, and walked aft again. I went below.

There was a shout of laughter from the men in the forecastle when I appeared. One of them patted me on the back.

"We'll make something of you, my lad," said one. "You'll turn out all right. Bill there was just like you at one time—and now he's the biggest cut-throat of us all!"

There was another laugh at this.

"Give the boy some grub," said another. "He looks half-dead."

They handed me a plate of boiled pork and a yam. I ate it hungrily, while I listened to the stream of frightful oaths that flowed from the lips of these godless men. Only one man kept silence, and that was the man they called Bill, who was nearly as big as the captain himself.

For the rest of the afternoon I was left to myself, but just after sunset one of the watch on deck bawled down the hatchway.

"Send that boy aft to the captain—sharp!"

"Do you hear, youngster? Look alive," said Bill, raising his great frame from the locker on which he had been asleep for the past two hours.

I went up the ladder, and went aft, where one of the men showed me into the cabin.

It was plainly furnished and lit by a lamp that hung from a beam. Seated on a camp stool at the table, studying a chart of the Pacific, was the captain. He looked up at me.

"What's you name?" he asked.

"Ralph Rover," I replied.

"How did you come to be on that island?"

I told him. He sat frowning for a moment when I had finished.

"I could use a lad like you," he said at last. "We might have treated you a little roughly, but that was because you gave us a bit of trouble. I'm no pirate, boy, but a lawful trader—a rough one, perhaps, but that can't be helped in these seas, where there are so many murderous black-guards. I trade in sandal-wood—and if you choose to be-have yourself I'll take you along with me and give you a share in the profits. You can look after the cabin and keep the log, and superintend the traffic on shore sometimes. What do you say? Would you like to be a trader?"

What *could* I say? I agreed to become one of the crew until we reached some spot where I might be put ashore.

When I left the cabin and went on deck my heart was still heavy within me. Whatever the captain said, I was quite sure that he and his men were far from being honest traders.

Chapter Thirteen
Bloodshed

Three weeks had passed.

I stood on the quarter-deck watching a shoal of porpoises swimming around the ship. There was a dead calm, with no cloud in the blue above and no breath of wind upon the blue below. The only sound was the slow creaking of the masts as we swayed on the swell, and an occasional flap of the hanging sails.

Most of the crew lay fast asleep under an awning that they had stretched across the foredeck. The man Bill was at the tiller, but he had so little to do that from time to time he took a little turn around the deck. At last he moved close to me and leaned on the rail at my side.

"Boy," he said suddenly, "this is no place for you."

"I know," I said. "But the captain said he'd put me ashore at the end of this trip."

"What else did he tell you?" asked Bill, lowering his voice.

"He said he was a trader, and told me he'd give me share of the profits if I joined the crew."

Bill scowled.

"He lied when he said that" he began, and was interrupted by a shout from the lookout.

"Sail ho!"

"Where away?" cried Bill, springing to the tiller.

"On the starboard quarter, hull down!"

The crew were stirring, startled by the sudden cry. The captain came on deck and climbed into the rigging to peer towards the horizon.

"Take in top-sails," he bawled, and swung himself back to the deck.

The men sprang into the rigging and went aloft like cats. All was movement and bustle. Topsails were taken in and stowed, the watch stood by the sheets and halyards, and the captain gazed anxiously for the breeze which was rushing towards us like a sheet of dark blue. A minute later it struck the ship. She trembled, then bent gracefully to the wind, cutting through the waves towards the strange sail.

Within half an hour we were close enough to see that she, too, was a schooner, and from the clumsy look of her masts and sails I judged her to be a trader. She did not seem to like the look of us, for the instant the breeze reached her she crowded all sail and showed us her stern. I could see, however, that we would soon overhaul her. When we were within half a mile we hoisted British colours, and the captain called for a shot to be put across her bows.

In a moment, to my surprise, a large portion of the bottom of the boat amidships was removed, and in the hole so exposed appeared an immense brass gun.

I gaped. I could hardly believe my eyes. The gun worked on a swivel and was raised by machinery. It was loaded and fired. A cannon-shot struck the water a few yards ahead of the ship we chased, then ricocheted into the air and plunged into the sea beyond.

It was enough. The ship ahead backed her top-sails and hove-to, while we ranged up and lay to about a hundred yards from her.

"Lower the boat," the captain ordered.

The boat was lowered and manned by a dozen of our men, all armed with cutlasses and pistols. As the captain walked past me, he said: "Jump into the stern-sheets, Ralph; I may want you."

I was surprised, but obeyed him. In less than ten minutes we were all standing on the stranger's deck, staring at her ragged crew. Every one of them was a black man all unarmed, and all quite clearly scared. Their captain was a tall, middle-aged man, dressed in a white cotton shirt, a swallow-tailed coat, and a straw hat, while his legs were bare below the knees.

He swept off his straw hat and made a low bow to our captain.

"Where do you come from? What cargo are you carrying?" our captain asked.

"We is come from Aitutaki," was the answer. "We was go for Rarotonga. We is native miss'nary ship, called de *Olive Branch*. De cargo is two tons coconuts, seventy pigs, twenty cats, an' de Gosp'l."

Our men roared with laughter at this, but the captain silenced them with a frown.

"Step into the cabin," he said to the missionary. "I want to have a talk with you."

The two were in the cabin for about a quarter of an hour, and shook hands in a friendly way when they came on

deck once more. The captain ordered us into our boat, and we returned to the schooner. Within half an hour we had left the other ship far behind.

That night I went on deck and found Bill at the helm alone.

"Tell me," I said to him, "is this ship really a trader?"

"Yes and no," he answered. "She does some trading, but she's just as much a pirate. She trades when she can't take by force, and she takes by force whenever she can. I've seen some pretty murderous things done on this deck."

"Then why did the captain let that ship escape this afternoon?"

"Because he wouldn't harm a missionary. He knows, like everybody else, that the only places in the South Seas where ships can put in without having trouble with the natives, are those where the people are Christian. The missionaries are useful, because they tame these wild islanders. In the untamed state they're a pretty savage lot, as you might find out, my lad."

Our track after this lay through a cluster of small islands, and a careful watch was kept, for we were not only in danger of being attacked by savages but we also ran some risk from the coral reefs that rose up in the channels between the islands.

We were becalmed one day close to a small island. Since we were in need of fresh water, the captain ordered the boat ashore to bring off a cask or two, and told me to go with the men.

We were quite close to the shore when a crowd of naked

natives came pelting out of the trees and gathered at the water's edge, waving spears and clubs in a threatening manner. We, of course, stopped rowing, while the mate stood up and made signs to the savages. They replied with a shower of heavy stones, one or two of which struck some of our men, cutting them rather badly. Instantly we levelled our muskets, but before we could put a volley over the savages' heads the captain hailed us from the ship.

"Don't fire! Pull off to the point behind you!"

We pulled away from the shore, now crowded with about five hundred shrieking savages. We had gone a couple of hundred yards when a loud roar thundered over the sea and the big brass gun on the schooner sent a hail of small-shot right into the living mass on the beach, mowing them down and cutting a wide lane right through them.

Those who were left alive let out a yell of terror and fled for the woods. Heaps of dead men, however, lay upon the sands. Among them I could see the wounded writhing and twisting in agony, while here and there one or two tried to stagger towards the woods and fell before they had taken a few steps.

My blood curdled at the horror of the things I saw. The captain's voice carried over the water.

"All right, lads. Pull ashore and fill your water-casks!"

We obeyed, all of us breathing hard, but I could feel that even the men were shocked by this ruthless act. We came to the mouth of a rivulet and found it streaming with blood. I was sickened by the thought of the many who were now dead and who had so recently been standing on its banks.

One body, which had been washed down, was jammed between two rocks, with staring eyeballs turned towards us and black hair waving in the ripples of the blood-red stream.

No one tried to stop our landing now. We carried the casks to a pool higher up, filled them, and pulled back to the ship. A breeze sprang up soon afterwards and carried us away from the dreadful spot—but nothing, I felt, would ever take away from me the memory of what I had seen.

Chapter Fourteen
The Island of Emo

At dusk, two days later, we found ourselves a few miles to the windward of a large island, from which rose a high, bare mountain peak. I asked Bill what it was called.

"That's Emo," he said. "I know it well. I've been there before, and so has this ship. It's famous for its sandal-wood and we've taken off many cargoes already—and paid for them, too! The savages are so many that the captain hasn't dared to take them by force. Even so, they don't like us very much. The last time we were here the men behaved very badly, and I wonder that the captain's come back to the place. If you ask me, we'll run into trouble here . . ."

We ran, next morning, inside a barrier reef and dropped our anchor in six fathoms of water, just opposite the mouth of a small creek. A big village lay about half a mile from this point.

The captain ordered a boat to be lowered and told me to follow him. We pulled ashore, taking with us fifteen men, all heavily armed, and with the big brass gun aimed to cover us.

A swarm of savages ran to meet us. With them came their chief, Romata, who led us up to his house, feasted us on baked pig, and talked for a long time with the captain, who spoke the native tongue.

I gathered from Bill that Romata had said he was glad to see us, and that he would set his men to work cutting down and loading sandal-wood trees for us. Romata, who was a huge man with a great black beard, was full of smiles and friendliness.

The next day most of our men were sent ashore to help cut the sandal-wood. I went with them, while the captain and one or two more stayed on board beside the brass gun, which they had trained point-blank at Romata's hut.

During the rest-hour Bill and I wandered down to the beach to watch the savages swimming in the surf. After a little while one of them came sweeping in on the crest of a wave and landed with a violent bound almost on the spot where we stood. As he rose panting to his feet I saw, to my great surprise, that he was Tararo—my old friend of the Coral Island!

We stared at each other. Then he gave a shout, rushed forward, took me by the neck, and rubbed his nose hard against mine.

"Has that chap taken a fancy to you?" asked Bill in some surprise. "Or is he an old friend?"

He spoke to Tararo in the native tongue, and the two held a long conversation, during which Tararo often pointed to me. When they paused I begged Bill to ask him about the girl Avatea, whom we had saved. At mention of her name, Tararo frowned darkly and his eyes flashed with anger. Bill listened to him for what seemed a long time.

"Tararo is on a visit to this island," said Bill at last. "He comes from an island called Mango, where the girl is now.

He's angry with her because he's picked out a man for her to marry and she won't do it. *She* wants to marry a chief who lives on another island. If she won't do what he wants when he goes back, he says he'll send her to her lover as a *long pig!*"

I gaped at him. His face was grim.

"What's that?" I asked.

"It means that he'll see her baked over a fire—just like a pig—then send her off to be eaten."

I could do no more than stare at him speechless and aghast.

We were another week at Emo and, as the days passed, it became clear that there was trouble brewing between Romata and the captain. Once they quarrelled on the shore and Romata threatened to send a fleet of his war-canoes to burn the schooner. The captain just smiled at this, looked the chief in the eye, and said: "Try it and see what happens. I've only to raise my little finger and my big gun will blow your whole village to pieces!"

Romata quietened down immediately, but I could see that he was seething with rage. It was, therefore, no surprise when he sent a message to the captain on the eighth day to say that we were not to send our men ashore. Only the captain was to go, because Romata had something to say to him.

The captain was gone for several hours and his face was as black as thunder when he returned. He shut himself up in the cabin, while the rest of us waited to see what would happen next.

That evening, when I was on deck, I heard part of a conversation between the captain and the mate. They were down in the cabin, but the skylight was off so that I heard every word quite clearly.

"I don't like it," said the mate, to begin with. "It seems to me that we'll have hard fighting and nothing to show for it."

"Nothing to show for it!" exclaimed the captain angrily. "There's a fine cargo lying in the woods and that blackguard chief knows it.

Now he says he won't let me take it off. Well, I'm going to show him a thing or two!"

"What are you going to do?" asked the mate.

"I'm going to have the schooner rowed up to the head of that creek over there and then creep through the woods to the village. These cannibals are always dancing around their fires at night, so we can drop forty or fifty at the first volley. After that the thing will be easy enough. The savages will take to the woods, we'll grab what we want, up anchor, and away. Give the men a glass or two of rum and warn them to be ready at midnight."

I'd heard enough. I crept away, awaiting the coming struggle with dread.

At midnight the men were mustered on deck, the cable was cut, and the schooner quietly rowed up into the creek. It took half an hour to reach the spot where the captain wanted us to land. Here a small kedge anchor, attached to a thin line, was let over the stern.

"Now, lads," whispered the captain, as he walked along

the line of men who stood ready, "don't be in a hurry, aim low, and don't waste your first shots."

Within a matter of minutes we were all ashore and lined up beneath the overhanging trees.

"There's no need to leave a man with the boat," I heard the mate whisper to the captain. "We shall want all hands. Let Ralph stay."

The captain ordered me to stand by and guard the boat. Then he glided off among the bushes, followed by the men.

I waited in the darkness, my heart throbbing wildly. For a long time there was no sound, and a feeling of dread slowly crept over me. I was sure that something terrible was about to happen.

And then I heard a shot.

It seemed to come from the village, and was followed at once by a chorus of shrieks and yells. Shot after shot rang out and echoed through the woods; there were more shouts and screams, and then the firing seemed to be going on all over the place, as if parties of men were scattering through the forest.

The noise went on for what seemed a very long time, and then I heard a long-drawn-out yell that could have come only from the savages. It sounded as if they were triumphant, and my blood ran cold at the thought. What should I do if our men were beaten? I could not let myself be taken by the savages; to flee to the mountains would be hopeless; and to take the schooner out of the creek without help was impossible.

I had just made up my mind to get back on board the

ship, when my blood was chilled by an appalling shriek. I knew the voice to be that of one of the crew. It was followed by a chorus of loud shouts from at least a hundred savage throats. Then came another shriek of agony, another, and another.

I waited no longer, but seized the boat-hook to push myself from shore. As the boat moved a man came crashing through the bushes, panting and sobbing for breath.

"Stop, Ralph!" cried a voice. "Wait for me!"

It was Bill. He bounded into the boat with a leap that almost upset her.

"Push off!" he gasped, and I did so readily enough.

In a matter of seconds we were on board the ship; the boat was made fast, the line of the anchor cut, and the oars run out. They were great sweeps that it took all my strength to pull, but, between us, we got the schooner under way.

We began to glide down the creek, but before we reached its mouth a yell from a thousand voices on the bank told us that we had been seen. I heard splashes as a number of the savages plunged into the water and swam towards us. One of them managed to grab hold of the cut rope dangling from the stern, and clambered up on to the deck. Bill let the fellow straighten up, then struck him a blow that sent him toppling back overboard.

But now a greater danger awaited us, for the savages had outrun us on the bank and were about to plunge into the water in front of the schooner.

I shouted to Bill. He came to his feet, drew a pistol from

his belt, sprang to the brass gun, held the pan of his pistol over the touch-hole, and fired. The flash and the crashing thunder of the gun burst upon the savages with such a deafening roar that it seemed as if the island had been torn asunder.

In that moment of surprise and hesitation we had time to pass the danger point. A breeze, which the woods of the shore had stopped us from feeling, caught and bulged out our sails. The ship bent before it and we were wafted out to sea.

Chapter Fifteen
The Return

Now that the danger was past I knew, quite suddenly, that I was completely worn out. I remember feeling the cool breeze upon my face as we left that hateful island behind us, and then I must have pitched forward and fallen asleep upon the deck.

When I awoke the sun was shining in my eyes. I sat up and stared round. I saw a calm sea and felt the schooner cutting through it with the help of a steady breeze. Bill was seated upon the deck behind me, his head laid upon his right arm, which was wrapped around the tiller. The slight noise I made as I lurched to my feet made him look up and see me there.

One look at his face and I sprang towards him in great anxiety. He was deadly pale. His hair, which hung in untidy locks over his face, was clotted with blood. Blood also stained his hollow cheeks and the front of his shirt, which was all torn and soiled with mud.

"Bill!" I cried. "You were wounded!"

He winced and nodded.

"Yes," he said quietly. "I've got an ugly wound, lad. I've been waiting for you to waken, to ask you to get me a drop o' brandy from the cabin locker."

I ran below at once, found the brandy, and brought back

some broken biscuits. He seemed a little better after he had eaten and taken a long drink of the brandy and water. Almost at once he fell asleep, and I watched him anxiously till he woke. He smiled at me when he did so.

"I feel better for that, Ralph," he said. Then he made to rise, but he sank back again with a deep groan.

"Lie still," I said. "I'll get you some proper food, and then take a look at your wound."

I left him, lighted a fire in the galley, cooked him some eggs, and made a pot of coffee. He managed to eat well enough. Then I helped him strip off his shirt and took a look at his wound.

It was a knife-wound, very deep, in the chest. It did not bleed much and I was in high hopes that it might not be serious. But Bill shook his head.

"Sit down, Ralph," he said, "and I'll tell you all about it. We didn't take the savages by surprise last night, as the captain had said we should. Romata must have expected us to try something like that, and he kept a good watch on us. The savages ambushed us before we'd got as far as the village. Ralph, there seemed to be thousands of them. The captain was stabbed almost at once. The rest of us scattered into the woods, with a mob of screaming savages on our heels. One of them caught up with me and we had a bit of a scrap, but he stabbed me before I put him down. There were more of them after me, but they weren't quick enough to stop me reaching the boat."

He paused, his face all drawn and tired.

"Bill," I said, "we've got to make up our minds what we

are going to do now. The wind's getting up. Which way shall we steer?"

He shook his head.

"It doesn't matter to me," he said. "I think my time's getting short. Go where you like."

"I think we'd better steer for the Coral Island. The captain once pointed it out to me on the chart, and I marked it afterwards. I think I can find it again. If you sit beside the tiller and steer for an hour or so each day, while I have a nap, we ought to manage between us."

Bill nodded.

"You know, Ralph," he said, "I've been a pirate three years now. I was kidnapped aboard this schooner, and kept here by force until I agreed to join the crew. I'm beginning to wish now that I'd lived a better life."

He sank back with a groan. A low hissing sound came sweeping across the sea. The wind had risen and now a squall was coming. I started to my feet, ran to shorten sail, then returned aft and took my stand at the helm.

The wind burst upon us in sudden, squally gusts and the spray was flying over the decks. The schooner sprang forward like a war-horse. Clouds had darkened the sky, and the wind began to whistle and shriek through the rigging. Quite suddenly the wind shifted a point. At once a heavy sea caught us on the bow and laid the ship over almost on her beam-ends.

Bill lost his hold of the belaying-pin which had served to steady him and slid with stunning violence against the skylight. I shouted to him, but he just lay still and I did not

dare to leave the tiller to go to his help. For an hour the blast drove us along, while the schooner dashed through the waves. Then the squall passed away and left us rocking on the lifting sea.

I dashed to Bill's side, dragged him into the cabin, and somehow managed to lift him on to the couch. I fetched the brandy-bottle, rubbed his face and hands with the stuff, and tried to pour a little down his throat. It was no use. At last I let go of the hand I had been rubbing. It dropped heavily to the deck. I put my hand over his heart, but could feel no flutter at all—Bill was dead.

I sat for some time, looking upon his pale, cold features. Then I rose, tied a cannon-ball to his feet, and, with feelings of the deepest sorrow, let him slide into the sea.

For fully a week after that a steady breeze blew out of the east. I managed to hoist the topsails, having lashed the helm to hold the schooner on her course. In this way, I was able to snatch a few hours' sleep whenever the sea was calm, and after a week of fair sailing I guessed that I must be drawing near to Coral Island.

On the evening of the fourteenth day I was wakened out of a nap by a loud cry. I started up, gazed around me, and was surprised and delighted to see a large albatross soaring over the ship.

Next morning, as I stood with heavy eyes at the helm, I waited anxiously for daylight, and peered towards the horizon, where I thought I saw something like a black cloud against the dark sky. Being always on the alert for squalls, I ran to the bow. There could be no doubt it was a squall,

and as I listened I thought I heard the murmur of the coming gale. At once I set to work to shorten sail. After an hour and a half I had most of it reduced and the day was dawning clear. I cast a glance ahead. I could hear the roar of the waves, and as a single ray of the rising sun gleamed over the ocean I saw—what! could it be that I was dreaming?—that magnificent breaker with its ceaseless roar!—that mountain-top!—yes, once more I beheld Coral Island!

Chapter Sixteen
The Last of the Coral Island

I shouted and cried with joy as I gazed towards the island. It was still many miles away but near enough for me to make out the outlines of the two mountains.

It would take me two or three hours to run the ship in. I knew that Jack and Peterkin were not in the habit of rising before six, and as it was now only three, I hoped to arrive before they were awake. I made up my mind to run the schooner into the lagoon and bring up opposite our old camp. The anchor was hanging at the cathead, so all I had to do was cut the tackling and down it would drop.

I searched among the flags until I found the terrible "Jolly Roger", which I ran up to the peak. While I was doing this, a thought struck me. I went the powder magazine, brought up a blank cartridge, and loaded the big brass gun. I took care to grease its mouth well, then went and thrust the poker into the fire.

All was now ready. I was not more than a quarter of a mile from the reef. In no time, it seemed, I was gliding through the entrance. On coming opposite the camp, I put the helm hard down. The schooner came round and lost way. I ran forward, let go the anchor, caught up the red-hot poker, put it to the brass gun, and shattered the morning silence with an almighty bang.

I gazed hopefully towards the shore.

Before the echoes had died away, I saw Peterkin bound out of the camp, his eyeballs starting from his head with surprise and terror. He gave one look, one yell, then fled into the bushes like a wild cat. The next moment Jack appeared, took one look, and turned to run.

I was almost mad with joy.

"Ahoy!" I shouted. "Peterkin! Jack! It's *me*!"

Jack came to a halt and turned. Peterkin appeared out of the bushes. I shouted again, and the two of them ran at full speed towards the beach. I could no longer contain myself. I threw off my jacket and jumped overboard at the same moment that Jack bounded into the sea. We met in deep water, clasped each other round the neck, and sank to the bottom. When we had struggled back to the surface, I say Peterkin spluttering about like a wounded duck, laughing and crying by turns, and choking himself with salt water.

How can I tell of the joy that followed by landing on the beach? We all of us acted like mad things, leaping and prancing and talking and shouting, and beating each other upon the back.

And then, of course, I had to tell my tale. As soon as I had finished the two of them made me go over it again. Both were very worried by what I could tell them of the probable fate of the girl Avatea. Jack clenched his teeth, shook his fist towards to sea, and said that he'd like to break Tararo's head.

After they had pumped me dry, it was my turn to ask

what had happened to them since I'd been gone, and how they had got out of the Diamond Cave.

"We waited an hour for you to come back," said Jack, "and then began to get really worried. I dived out of the cave by myself, and there was no sign of you or anyone else. Then I saw the schooner standing out to sea, and decided that the pirates must have carried you away with them. You can guess how I felt then. I dived back to the cave and told Peterkin. We had to think of a way of getting out without your help. As far as I could see, there was only one way it could be done. I dived out, found a good strong pole, took it back with me, and lashed Peterkin to it to keep him straight and stiff—"

"You can imagine how much I liked *that*!" said Peterkin. Jack grinned.

"We searched all over the island for you," he went on, "and felt pretty low when we knew for certain the pirates had carried you off. And then, when we were out on the reef one day, Peterkin saw a small, dark object lying among the rocks. We found that it was a small keg of gunpowder."

"I sent you that," I put in, with a smile.

"Well, we found it very useful," said Jack, "and we've been able to use the pistol ever since. But the island became a dreary place after you'd gone, and we were longing for a ship to take us off. Now that we've got it, I think we ought to have a look at some of the other islands of the South Seas. We couldn't really do much better than shape our course for the island on which Avatea lives, and see if we can do anything to rescue her."

There was a little silence while we stared at him and thought this over. Then Peterkin and I spoke together.

"Good idea!" we said. "We'll come!"

It was settled. We lost no time in making ready to leave the island. As the ship was already laden with stores, we had very little to do.

When all was ready, we climbed to the mountain-top and gazed for the last time at the rich green valleys, the white sandy beach, the still lagoon, and the coral reef with its crested breakers.

We went back to the camp, and carved our names upon a piece of board, which we set up upon the shore. A few minutes later we were on board the schooner.

A steady breeze was blowing when we set sail, a little before sunset. It carried us past the reef and out to sea. The shore grew rapidly more indistinct as the shades of evening fell, while our ship bounded lightly over the waves. Slowly the mountain-top sank on the horizon until it became a mere speck. In another moment the sun and our Coral Island sank together into the broad bosom of the Pacific.

Chapter Seventeen
The Island of Mango

We made good speed. For three weeks the breeze blew fair, and at the end of that time we arrived off the island of Mango, to which Tararo was the chief. Beating up for the south side of the island, we arrived before sunset and hove-to off the coral reef.

No sooner were we anchored than a canoe put off from the shore. As it drew close we saw in it a mild-looking native, about forty years of age, who came on board and made us a low bow. He was dressed in European clothes and wore a straw hat.

"Good day, gentlemen," he said. "Welcome to the island of Mango. I am the missionary teacher at this station."

"You're the very man we want to see, then," said Jack. "Come down to the cabin, and let's have a talk."

We learned from the missionary that the people of the island were divided into two groups Christians and heathens. Avatea lived among the heathens though she really wished to join the Christians, but Tararo would not let her. The poor girl had fallen in love with a Christian chief, who lived on an island about fifty miles to the south. Besides this, we learned that the heathens were at war among themselves, and that Tararo's side had won a great victory in a battle fought that very day.

When the missionary went back to the shore, we took the schooner in through the passage in the reef, and anchored off a village at the head of a small bay.

The next day, when we went ashore, we were given a warm welcome by the missionary and his wife, who led us to their hut and set before us a meal of baked meats and fruit. When we had eaten, we asked the missionary if he could find us a crew for the schooner. This he did easily enough, so we made up our minds to sail round the island at once and drop anchor opposite the heathen village. When we sailed, a few hours later, the missionary himself came with us.

After only two hours' sailing, we dropped about a hundred yards off the heathen village, and fired our big gun by way of salute. The excitement and commotion on shore showed us that we had struck terror into the hearts of the natives: but seeing that we did not offer to molest them, they at last sent a canoe out towards us. The missionary spoke to the men who manned it and told them that we were friends. He also said that we wished to speak with their chief, and that we should like him to come on board.

The canoe put back to the shore, but shortly returned with the message that Tararo could not come on board that day, since he was busy with certain religious ceremonies before the gods. He therefore begged us to land and visit him, and this we decided to do.

On reaching the beach we were received by a crowd of naked savages, who shouted a wild welcome and led us to a hut where a baked pig was quickly prepared for us. When

we had eaten, we asked that we might be taken to Tararo but were told that he was just going to the temple of his gods and could not see us yet.

"Well," said Jack, rising, "if he won't come to see me, then I'll go and see him." He turned to the missionary. "Will you come too?" he asked.

The missionary shook his head.

"I cannot," he said. "I will have nothing to do with their heathen gods."

This we could understand, so the three of us set off without him. Jack led us through some banana groves to rising ground immediately behind the village, on top of which stood the temple, under the dark shade of a group of ironwood trees.

As we followed the broad path that climbed the hill we heard the shouts of a great crowd coming from behind. We drew aside into the bushes and awaited their coming up. Soon we saw them—a long procession of natives dancing and shrieking in the most frantic manner. All of them were daubed and smeared with paint. In their midst came a band of men, carrying three or four planks, on which were seated more than a dozen men.

Only when they drew very close did the awful truth dawn upon me. All the men upon the planks were dead, but tied up in a sitting position. They were, we learned later, men who had been killed in battle the day before. They were now on their way to be presented to the gods, and then eaten. As they bent their sightless eyes and grinning mouths over the dancing crew below, it was as if they laughed in

ghastly mockery at the utter inability of their enemies to hurt them any more.

Behind the procession came a shrieking crowd of women and children, with whom we mingled and whom we followed to the temple.

It was a tall, round building open at one side. Around it were strewn heaps of human bones and skulls. At a long table inside sat the priest, an old man with a grey beard, and before him lay several knives with which he performed his office of dissecting dead bodies.

The bodies were arranged before the temple in a sitting position. A man, called an orator, advanced, and, laying his hands on their heads, began to chide them in a low, bantering tone. We did not understand a word, but as he went on his voice grew louder. Then he shouted to them at the top of his lungs and finished up by kicking the bodies over and running away, amid the shouts and laughter of the people. They now rushed forward and dragged the bodies into the temple to be dissected by the priest before being taken out to be baked.

But we had seen enough. We were all pale and haggard as we hurried back to rejoin the missionary, who was equally sickened and distressed when he had heard our tale.

Before long, however, Tararo came along the beach, followed by a long line of men who bore baskets of fruit and vegetables on their heads. We walked to meet him, and he showed much pleasure at seeing us.

"And what is it that my friends wish to say?" he asked.

The missionary explained that we had come to ask him to spare Avatea's life.

Tararo frowned at this, and then replied at some length.

"He will not hear of this thing," the missionary told us. "He says the girl must die."

It was Jack's turn to frown.

"Tell him that if he does not do as I ask it will be the worse for him," he said fiercely. "Say that my big gun upon the ship will blow his village into the sea if he does not give up the girl."

"What does my friend say?" asked the chief, who seemed nettled by Jack's looks of defiance.

"He is displeased," replied the missionary.

Tararo scowled, and walked away towards the men who had carried the baskets, which they had emptied on to the beach in an enormous pile. A moment later two more men appeared, leading a young girl between them. They walked up to the heap of fruit and vegetables and placed her on the top of it. We all started, for the girl was Avatea.

The missionary grabbed Jack by the arm.

"We are too late, " he said hoarsely. "They are going to sacrifice her *now!*"

Chapter Eighteen
The Flight

We stood rooted to the earth with thick-coming fears. Then Jack gave a fierce shout, dashed aside two natives who stood in his way, rushed towards the heap, sprang up its side, and seized Avatea in his arms. He leaped down again and placed her back to a large tree. Then, wrenching a war-club from the hand of one of the savages, he whirled it above his head and yelled, his whole face blazing with fury:

"Come on, the lot of you, and do your worst!"

The savages gave an answering yell, and started towards him, but Tararo sprang forward and raised his hands above his head. The savages stopped and the chief turned to Jack.

"You are very brave—but foolish," he said. "But I do not forget that once you helped me. I will say that Avatea shall not be harmed for three days. Now go back to your ship."

"Do as he says," the missionary whispered to Jack. "Three days are worth having."

Jack hesitated for a moment, then lowered his club, and threw it to the ground. The missionary stepped forward and whispered a few words to Avatea. She replied by a single glance of her dark eyes, before Tararo took her by the hand and led her away.

We returned to the schooner. As soon as we were in the cabin, the missionary said,

"If you are prepared to give up this ship, the girl may yet be saved."

"How?" we asked eagerly.

"If you were to raise the anchor," the missionary said, "you'd have a thousand warriors standing on your deck. They will watch you all the time, so the ship must be left behind. These savages will think that you would not sacrifice it for the sake of a girl, so as long as the ship does not move all will be well. Now, I have told you that there is an island about fifty miles to the south. I suggest that you load a canoe with stores, put Avatea on board, and paddle to the island. I will stay here till they discover that you are gone."

"And what next then?" Jack asked.

"I do not know. At all events, I have told the girl to meet us at a spot to which I will guide you tonight. No watch will be kept on the girl, for they will think it impossible for her to escape. It will be easy for me to get hold of a canoe, but fifty miles on the open sea will not be an easy voyage to make."

"There's no other way," said Jack, and looked at Peterkin and me. "Do we go?" he asked.

We nodded. It was agreed.

It was close on midnight when we dropped over the side of the schooner and into the canoe which the missionary had sent one of the crew to get. We paddled quietly across the bay. A quarter of an hour brought us to an overhanging cliff. As the canoe grated on the beach a hand was laid upon the bow and a dim form was seen.

"Avatea?" whispered the missionary.

There was a soft murmur in the darkness, and the girl stepped into the canoe.

We sped once more across the still waters of the lagoon and put the missionary on board the schooner again. Then we turned towards the opening in the reef and drove the canoe into the long swell of the ocean.

All that night and the whole of the following day we plied the paddles in turn. Jack had taken the bearing of the island just after we started, and kept a pocket-compass before him as he paddled. Peterkin and I were in the bow, and Avatea worked untiringly in the middle.

At dusk of the next day, Jack threw down his paddle and called a halt.

"We've come a long way," he said. "It's time we had a good meal and a sound sleep."

We hungrily ate the cold roast pig we had brought with us, while the night closed in and all around was calm and dark and silent. And then we slept . . .

I was awakened by a cry from Peterkin, just as the grey dawn began to glimmer in the east.

"What's wrong?" said Jack, starting up.

"Look!" gasped Peterkin.

His face was filled with dread and he pointed across the sea. A glance showed me a great war-canoe speeding towards us. With a cry of despair Jack seized his paddle and shouted for us to do the same. We did not need telling. Already our four paddles were glancing in the water, and the canoe went bounding over the glassy sea.

The chase, however, could end only in one way. It was two hours before the war-canoe was close enough for us to hear the cries of the men in it, but then they came on rapidly.

Jack shouted for us to stop paddling. We turned the side of the canoe towards our enemies, and put down the paddles. Jack said nothing, but stood up and lifted his club in an attitude of bold defiance.

The other canoe came on like a war-horse, with the foam curling up from its sharp bow, and the spearheads of the savages gleaming in the sunlight. No one spoke. We could hear the hissing water, and see the fierce faces of the warriors as they came rushing on. I waited for them to turn the head of the canoe. They made no move to do so, and suddenly I realized their intention. I grasped my paddle, stood up, and gave one cry. Next moment the sharp prow of the war-canoe struck us like a thunderbolt and hurled us into the sea.

I'm not sure what happened after that, for I was struck on the head by the canoe in passing, went into the sea, and almost drowned. When I recovered my senses I found myself on my back, bound hand and foot, in the bottom of the large canoe. Peterkin and Jack were beside me.

The voyage back to Mango was one long torment. We were given neither food nor water the whole time and suffered agonies from thirst, for the air was exceptionally hot and it seemed that a storm was building up.

While we were being led ashore, we caught a glimpse of Avatea, who was not bound in any way. Our captors drove

us before them towards the hut of Tararo. The chief awaited us with an ugly look on his face. He spoke, his eyes flashing with anger, to the missionary, who stood beside him.

"My friends," said the missionary quietly, "Tararo says that his debt to you is cancelled. You must die."

Tararo signed to several of his men, who seized hold of Jack and Peterkin and me and dragged us through the bush to the edge of the village. Here they thrust us into a cave in the cliff, and, having barricaded the entrance, left us in total darkness.

We felt about for some time—for our legs were free, although our wrists were still bound—till we found a low ledge of rock running along one side of the cave. On this we seated ourselves and waited quietly for the end that we knew must be near.

At last we heard a noise at the entrance to the cave. The barricade was dragged away; then three savages entered and led us through the forest, towards the temple that stood on the hill. We had not gone far when a procession of natives came to meet us, shouting and beating drums. We were placed at the head of the procession and forced along towards the temple where, we knew, human beings were offered for sacrifice.

I staggered on, so lost in fear and horror that I was hardly aware that the sky had darkened.

Suddenly there came a growl of thunder overhead, and heavy drops of rain began to fall; the air was filled with the rush of something, and then the afternoon went mad . . .

A hurricane hit Mango with a deafening roar. The natives fled for shelter on every side, leaving us alone in the midst of the howling storm.

The wind caught us and whirled us along, while great, driven raindrops slapped hard against our flesh.

"Get down!" I heard Jack shout, and I threw myself to the ground.

A body sprawled down beside me. It was the missionary, and he had a knife in his hand.

"Thank the Lord," he cried, as he cut our bonds, "I am in time! Now, follow me."

We fought our way along in the teeth of the howling wind, which burst with the noise of a thunderclap among the trees, tearing many from their roots and hurling them to the ground. Rain cut across the land in sheets; lightning played like forked serpents in the air; and high above the roar of the storm thunder crashed and rolled in awful majesty.

We found shelter in a cave and stayed there all through that night and the next day, while the storm raged in fury. In the village the scene was appalling. Houses were blown down and whirled away. Great waves came sweeping in from the mighty ocean, rising higher and higher on the beach, until the sea was lashing its angry waters far inland and had dashed into wreck those few houses that were still standing.

A little before dawn on the second day the backbone of the hurricane broke. When the sun rose, the wind was no more than a steady breeze, and the sea had gone down

again. For the first time in two days we thought of the dangers from which we had been rescued by the storm.

"You must have food," the missionary told us. "I will get that for you, and then you must try to escape."

He went off, and was gone for a long time while we waited restlessly. At last we heard footsteps at the entrance, and the missionary stood there with his back to the light so that we could not see his face. As we moved towards him, he took Jack by the shoulders and exclaimed:

"My dear young friend, through the great goodness of God you are free!"

"Free!" we cried together.

"Yes, free—to come and go as you will. I warned Tararo that if he tried to kill you, then the Lord would punish him and all his people. The hurricane came to prove my words. Tararo has become a Christian, and his people are burning their gods of wood. Come and see for yourselves!"

We could scarcely believe our senses. Our eyes were dazzled by the bright sunshine, and our minds by what he had said, as we followed him from the cave and into the shambles of the village. One after another the savages rushed towards us and shook us by the hand. Then they fell in behind us, and, forming a sort of procession, we went to meet Tararo.

The chief was kindness itself, ready to do anything to help us; and Avatea, he promised, should be sent in a war-canoe to the island of her lover-chief.

Our next thought was for the schooner, which, we found, had been washed ashore but not seriously damaged by

the storm. With the help of Tararo's people we got her afloat again, and repaired what little damage she had suffered. Within a week she was fit for the open sea.

During this time the natives had started building a church, under the guidance of the missionary, and several rows of new cottages were marked out, so that the place soon looked as if it might well become as peaceful and beautiful a village as any in the South Sea Islands.

We now resolved to delay our departure no longer. Three natives volunteered to go with us to Tahiti, where we thought it likely that we should be able to pick up a crew of sailors to man our vessel.

It was a bright clear morning when we hoisted the snow-white sails of the pirate schooner and left the shores of Mango. The missionary and thousands of the natives came down to bid us God-speed, and to see us sail away. As the vessel bent before a light, fair wind, we glided quickly over the lagoon under a cloud of canvas.

That night, as we sat at the stern of the schooner gazing out upon the wide sea, a thrill of joy, strangely mixed with sadness, passed through our hearts; for we were at length "homeward bound", and were leaving far behind us the beautiful, bright green coral islands of the Pacific Ocean.